SQUID MONSTER

By Jill Eggleton
Illustrated by Richard Hoit

Rigby

SQUID MONSTER

It was November 4. Fran Stellar and Tomas Rankin were diving buddies. They were going cave-diving at the Blue Holes.

Fran and Tomas had explored the most beautiful diving places in the world. They had seen fish as small as pinheads, and monstrous fish as big as buses.

They had seen coral with amazing colors and strange shapes. They had swum in forests of seaweed as tall as skyscrapers. They had seen shipwrecks lying like white ghosts on the sandy ocean floor.

The underwater world was full of beauty, but there were hazards. Many dangerous creatures lived under the sea. Fran and Tomas knew not to disturb these creatures; after all, they were the invaders in the underwater world.

. . . . AS BIG AS BUSES

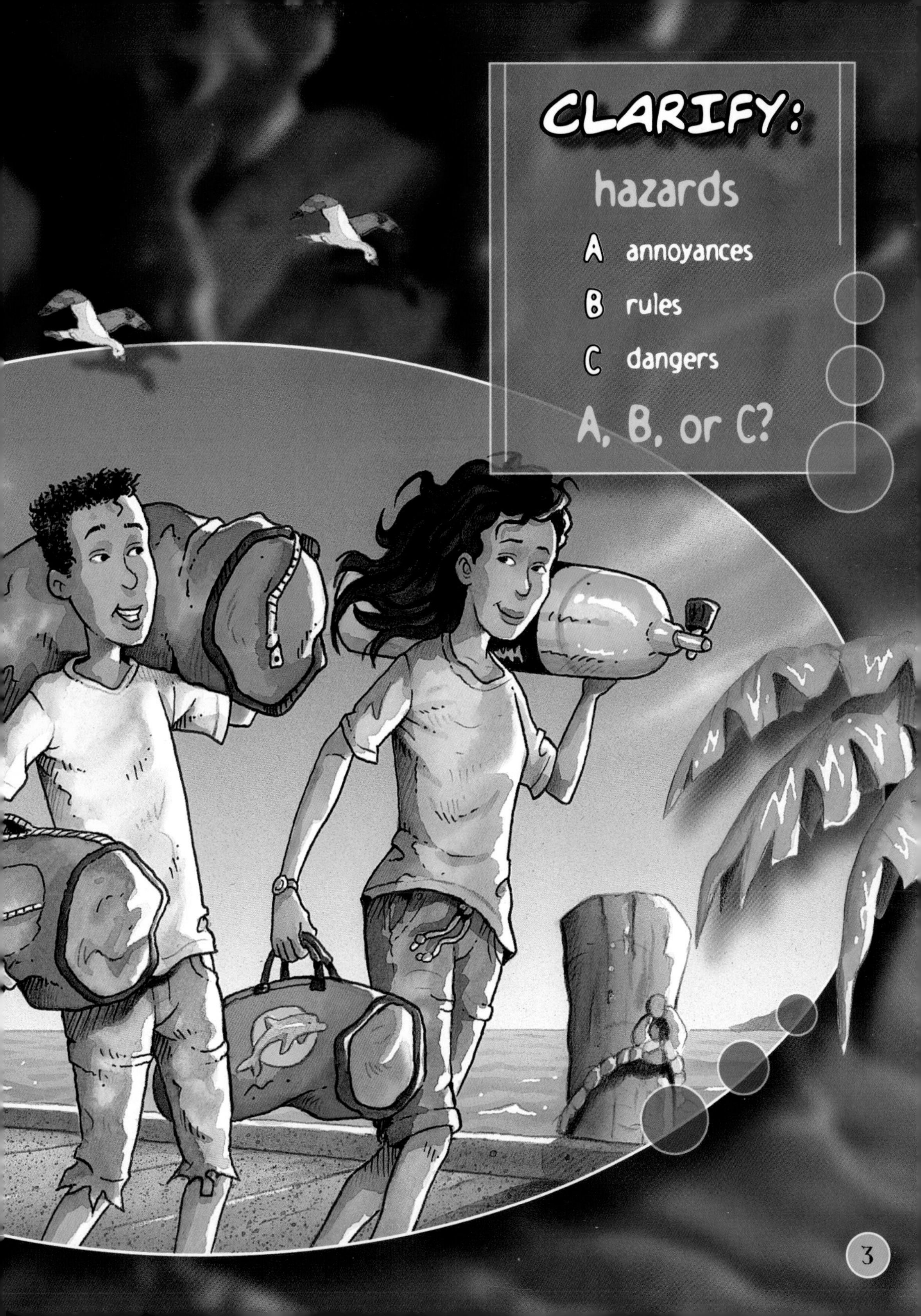
CLARIFY:
hazards
A annoyances
B rules
C dangers
A, B, or C?

Fran and Tomas had swum with sharks, but they had never been attacked. They had seen deadly jellyfish with long, floating tentacles, ready to paralyze and devour anything that crossed their path. But they had never been stung. They had been lucky!

Fran and Tomas had learned to be careful, always alert! They had prepared for their dive at the Blue Holes for weeks. This was a new experience and they were excited. They knew the mysterious Blue Holes were formed during the Ice Age, and were one of the most exciting places to dive in the world.

They had heard about beautiful caves of stalagmites and stalactites full of amazing sea creatures. They had heard about the fish in this underwater world that were more colorful than a jungle of birds.

Diving at the Blue Holes was very challenging. There were dangers – sharks and fierce water currents that could suck a diver into a cave like a cork down a drain. And . . . there was the fear of the sea monsters!

The people who lived near the Blue Holes talked about the legend of these monsters. "Terrible creatures," said Old Jack Dorman.

Old Jack had lived near the Blue Holes for years, and he loved to tell the story of the shipwrecked sailor. "His boat had sunk," he told Fran and Tomas. "He was clinging to a tiny raft . . . when all of a sudden, out from the depths of the sea, came this monstrous squid. It lunged at the tiny raft. The raft shattered like a fragile shell. The monster threw a huge, rubbery tentacle around the sailor's body, like a python snake grabbing its prey, and dragged him away. Nobody ever saw him again," said Old Jack, shaking his shaggy head. "I wouldn't be diving down there if I were you!"

SIMILE:

A simile compares one thing to another by using the words "like" or "as", and often creates a mental picture in the reader's mind.

Can you find a simile?

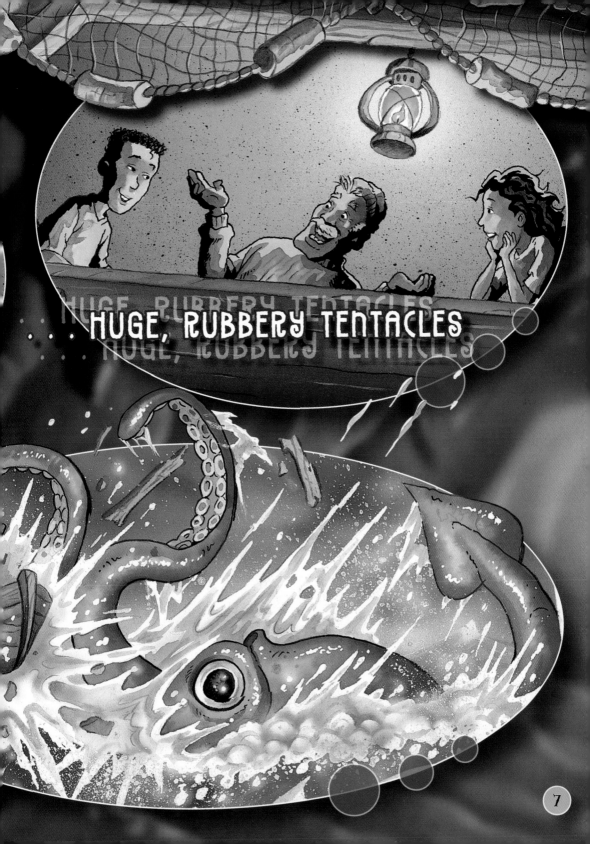

HUGE, RUBBERY TENTACLES

Fran and Tomas laughed. They knew the legend was just a story, told and retold, a story that had never proved to be true.

As they set off for their dive into the Blue Holes, Old Jack's story of the sea monster was quickly forgotten. The still, blue pool above the entrance to the Blue Holes beckoned them invitingly. They lowered themselves into the water. For a moment they floated, feeling relaxed. It was like being in a warm bath. Then Tomas said, "Let's go!"

QUESTION:

Why do you think Tomas and Fran quickly forgot about the story of the sea monster?

Fran let off the line. She and Tomas never went cave-diving without a line. It was a safeguard. They may need it to pull themselves out. It would be easy to get lost in the myriad of tunnels.

Tomas dived first. He looked back and saw Fran descending like a parachutist floating through the sky. They dived deeper, letting out the line as they went. The sun's rays gave the cave a **mysterious glow**. Fran and Tomas peered into nooks and crannies, excited as kids at a fair. But at this fair, all the shows were free!

A MYSTERIOUS GLOW

A MYSTERIOUS GLOW
A MYSTERIOUS GLOW

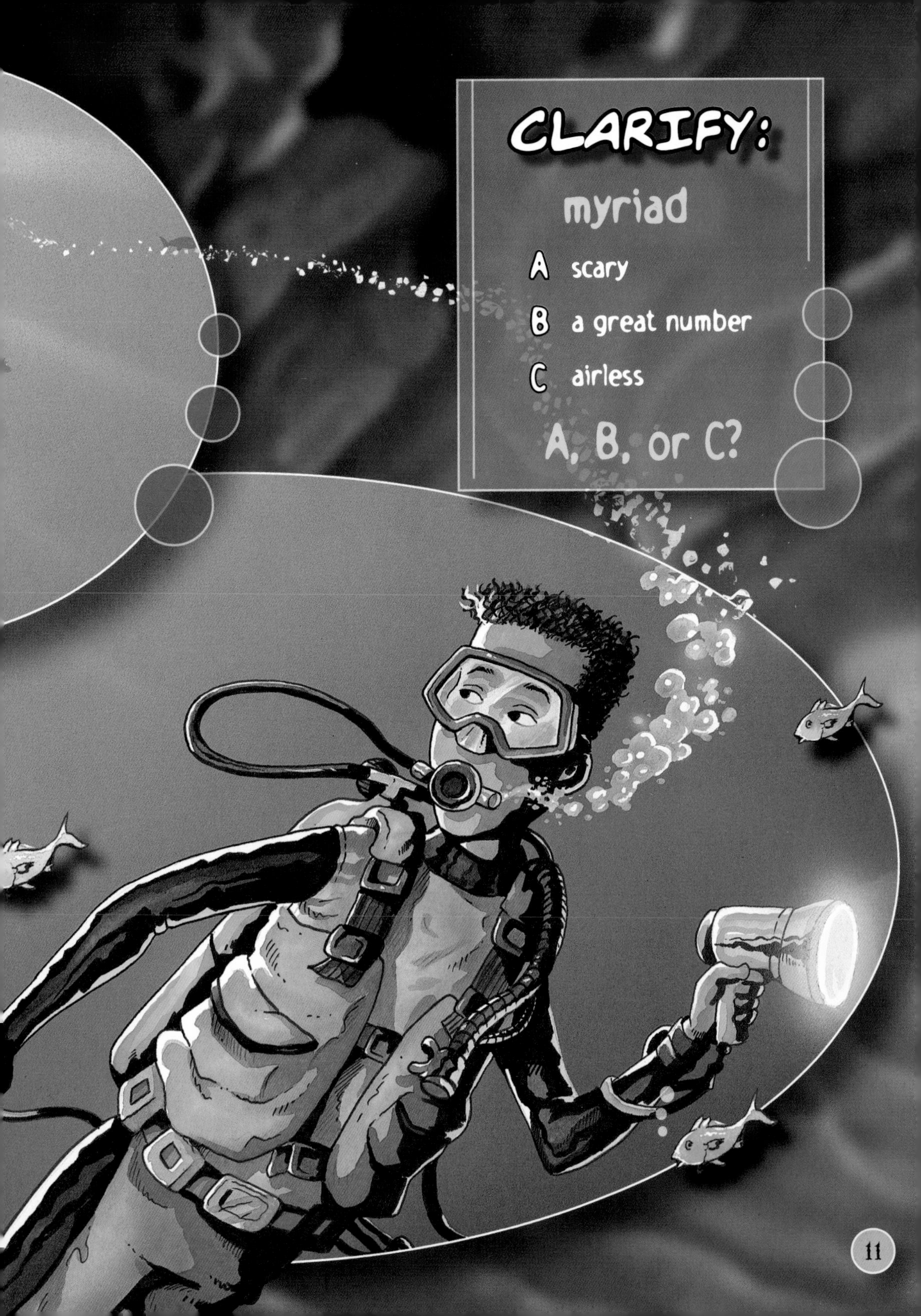

CLARIFY:

myriad

A scary

B a great number

C airless

A, B, or C?

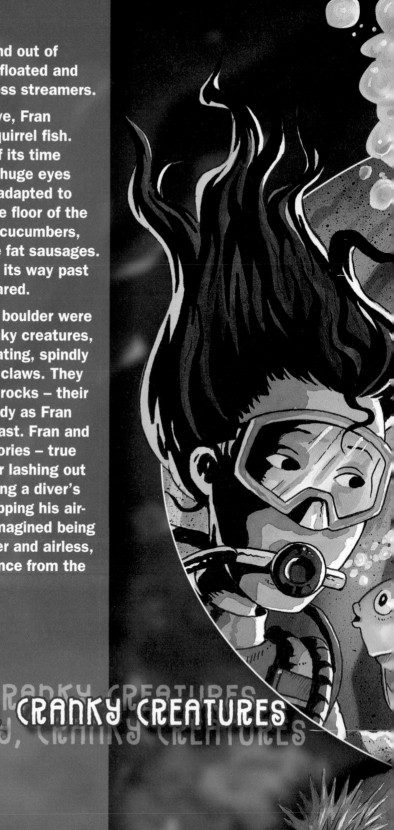

Tiny fish flitted in and out of the cave, and ferns floated and wavered like colorless streamers.

At the back of a cave, Fran and Tomas saw a squirrel fish. It had spent most of its time in the cave, and its huge eyes showed that it had adapted to the darkness. On the floor of the cave, they saw sea cucumbers, crawling around like fat sausages. A snake-eel weaved its way past them, then disappeared.

Behind nearly every boulder were lobsters – ugly, cranky creatures, with horny armor plating, spindly legs, and menacing claws. They burrowed under the rocks – their big claws at the ready as Fran and Tomas drifted past. Fran and Tomas had heard stories – true stories – of a lobster lashing out with a claw, snatching a diver's mouthpiece and snipping his air-supply hose! They imagined being deep under the water and airless, and kept their distance from the cranky lobsters.

UGLY, CRANKY CREATURES

QUESTION:

What do you think is meant by

". . . its huge eyes showed that it had adapted to the darkness"?

Fran and Tomas floated in and out of the tunnels and caves, and in and out of the stalagmites and stalactites that were covered in clinging seaplants. It was a wonderful feeling to be warm and weightless in a three-dimensional playground. There was always something new to look at. Each creature had its territory – its home.

After what seemed like just a few minutes in the tunnels and caves, Tomas looked at his air supply. It was time to leave. He tugged on the rope and signaled to Fran.

TIME TO LEAVE
TIME TO LEAVE
TIME TO LEAVE

PREDICT:

What do you think might happen in the story now?

They had just begun to ascend, when Tomas saw it – the giant squid.

The squid was staring at them with its human-like eyes. Tomas could see its eight arms with rows of suckers and tooth-like horny rings. He could see its tentacles. They were like long stretchy rubber cables. Was this the legendary monster? Tomas felt his body shivering, cold and clammy inside his thick diving suit. He tugged on the rope again and signaled frantically to Fran.

EMOTIONS:

What words would you use to describe how Tomas is feeling now?

desperate   anxious
angry   terrified   cross
sad   calm   unhappy

... HUMAN-LIKE EYES

Fran looked back. Tomas could see her eyes behind the glass mask, growing wide with fear. She began to ascend quickly. But not quickly enough.

The giant squid whipped out a tentacle, like a rodeo rider lassoing a calf. The tentacle wrapped around Fran's body. Then out whipped another one and clamped onto her shoulder, like a vice onto wood. Fran clung desperately to the rope, her face a mask of horror. The squid held on, trying to pull her into its writhing nest of arms.

EMOTIONS:

What words would you use to describe how Fran is feeling now?

desperate   anxious
angry   terrified   cross
sad   calm   unhappy

WRITHING NEST OF ARMS

19

For a moment Tomas was frozen in terror. This was not a legend. This was for real. Fran was in terrible danger.

Tomas reached for his diving knife. He had never used his diving knife to fend off a sea creature before, but this was a matter of life or death. His hand clasped the handle, twisting it in its sheath. Then he looked up. Towering above him was a rocky ledge. On the rocky ledge he saw a large stalactite that had broken off the cave roof. It lay there like an abandoned giant spear. Tomas knew he wouldn't be able to throw it with much force through the water, but maybe it might distract the squid and make it loosen its grip.

A MATTER OF LIFE OR DEATH

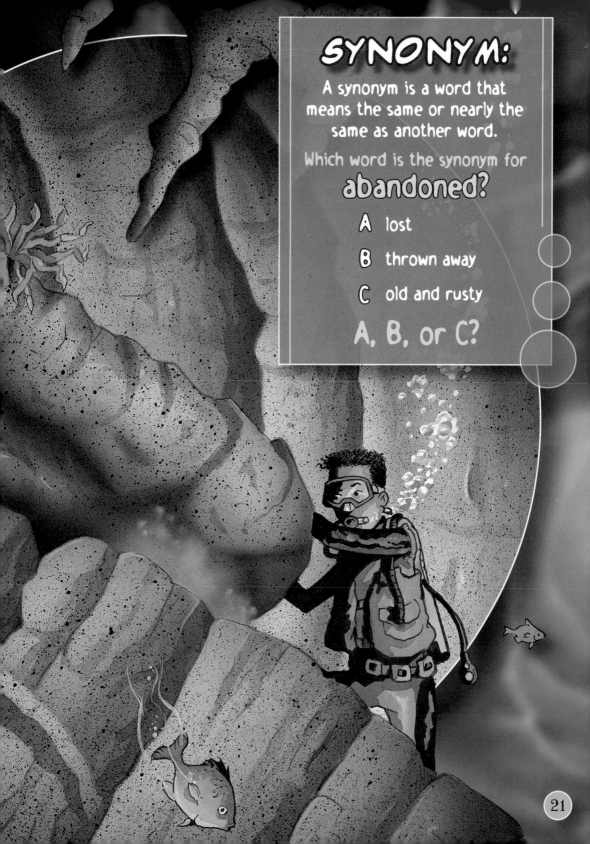

SYNONYM:

A synonym is a word that means the same or nearly the same as another word.

Which word is the synonym for

abandoned?

A lost

B thrown away

C old and rusty

A, B, or C?

21

Tomas carefully swam upward. He could feel the squid staring at him with eyes as large as dinner plates. It still had six free tentacles. Any moment, one could whip out and wrap him in its deadly grip! Tomas swam up. Fran saw him swimming away. She looked helpless, terrified. Her eyes pleaded . . . "Don't leave me!"

Tomas reached the rocky ledge. He put his flippered feet against the rock wall and heaved on the huge stalactite. It rolled off the ledge and drifted down toward the sneering squid. Would the stalactite connect with its target?

Tomas perched on the rock ledge, his heart pounding. The stalactite drifted down. Then thump – it hit the squid between its staring eyes.

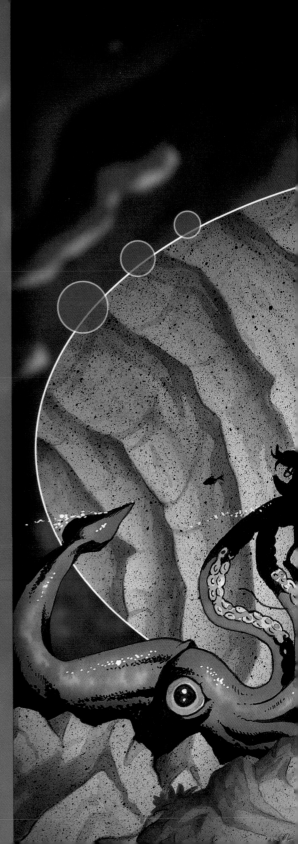

ACTION AND CONSEQUENCE:

Tomas heaved on the stalactite ...	It rolled off the ledge and drifted down toward the sneering squid.
The stalactite hit the squid ...	**?**

The squid jerked and reeled back. Its huge cylindrical body pulsated. Clouds of black ink oozed out. The squid's tentacles slackened their grip. Fran saw her chance.

Wriggling and squirming, Fran kicked with her flippers. Then she shot upward – free! Not waiting to look back, Fran grabbed the rope and swam up as fast as she could. Tomas was so close behind, Fran's flippers were brushing his face. He was afraid that at any moment the giant squid would come rocketing through the water after them. He knew that squids could overtake anything that swam.

But the squid was somewhere back in the depths . . . dizzy in its inky water.

INFERENCE:

What inference can be made about the speed of a giant squid?

BLACK INK OOZED OUT

Fran and Tomas surfaced. The sun had never looked so bright, or the sky so blue. They took off their masks and stared at each other. Their breath was coming in short, shallow gasps. Fran had been in the arms of the sea's most bizarre and terrifying creature. Finally Tomas spoke. His voice was thin and wheezy.

"That monster of the Blue Holes," he said, "is no legend!"

no LEGEND!

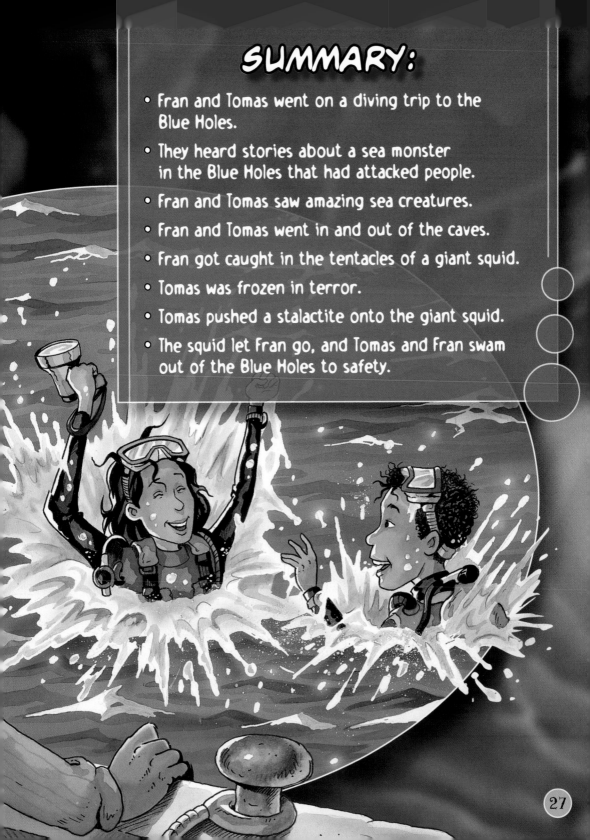

SUMMARY:

- Fran and Tomas went on a diving trip to the Blue Holes.

- They heard stories about a sea monster in the Blue Holes that had attacked people.

- Fran and Tomas saw amazing sea creatures.

- Fran and Tomas went in and out of the caves.

- Fran got caught in the tentacles of a giant squid.

- Tomas was frozen in terror.

- Tomas pushed a stalactite onto the giant squid.

- The squid let Fran go, and Tomas and Fran swam out of the Blue Holes to safety.

THINK ABOUT THE TEXT

Making connections – What connections can you make to the text?

feeling scared

having friends

feeling relief

TEXT-TO-SELF

having respect

experiencing panic

being well-prepared

having appreciation for nature

TEXT-TO-TEXT

Talk about other stories you may
have read that have similar features.
Compare the stories.

TEXT-TO-WORLD

Talk about situations in the world
that might connect to elements
in the story.

PLANNING A FACTUAL RECOUNT

1   Select a real event or experience.

2   Make a plan.

Think about:

Who

When

. . . It was November 4

Where

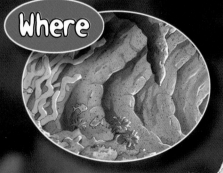

What

Think about events in order of sequence:

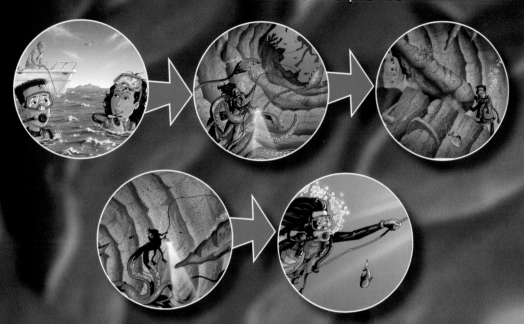

3 Include personal comments and thoughts
on events throughout your recount,
and a final comment.

Final comment

Finally Tomas spoke. His voice
was thin and wheezy.

"That monster of the Blue Holes,"
he said, "is no legend!"

A FACTUAL RECOUNT USUALLY . . .

A   Uses descriptive language

B   Uses the past tense for recording events

C   Contains a record of personal observations

D   Contains a record of interpretation of events

E   Uses words of time to connect events,
such as *first, next, then, during,* and *while*